KU-754-504

Contents

Alice
in Wonderland

PUFFIN BOOKS

Published by the Penguin Group
Penguin Books Ltd, 80 Strand, London WC2R 0RL, England
Penguin Group (USA), Inc., 375 Hudson Street, New York, New York 10014, USA
Penguin Books Australia Ltd, 250 Camberwell Road, Camberwell, Victoria 3124, Australia
Penguin Books Canada Ltd, 10 Alcorn Avenue, Toronto, Ontario, Canada M4V 3B2
Penguin Books India (P) Ltd, 11 Community Centre, Panchsheel Park, New Delhi – 110 017, India
Penguin Group (NZ), cnr Airborne and Rosedale Roads, Albany, Auckland 1310, New Zealand
Penguin Books (South Africa) (Pty) Ltd, 24 Sturdee Avenue, Rosebank 2196, South Africa

Penguin Books Ltd, Registered Offices: 80 Strand, London WC2R 0RL, England

www.penguin.com

First published 2004
1

Set in Linotype Cochin
Typeset by Rowland Phototypesetting Ltd, Bury St Edmunds, Suffolk

Made and printed in England by Clays Ltd, St Ives plc

British Library Cataloguing in Publication Data
A CIP catalogue record for this book is available from the British Library

ISBN 0–141–31774–4

Alice
in Wonderland

Narinder Dhami

PUFFIN

Also in the
Disney Classics *series:*

101 DALMATIANS
THE ARISTOCATS
BAMBI
LADY AND THE TRAMP
THE JUNGLE BOOK
THE LION KING
PINOCCHIO

Chapter One

It was a very hot day. Alice and her sister were resting under the shade of a leafy tree. Alice's sister was reading aloud from a history book, while Alice climbed up the tree and perched on a branch with her kitten, Dinah. She began to make a daisy chain.

'Alice!' said her sister crossly, as a foot swung in front of her.

'Hmm?' Alice glanced down dreamily. She saw her sister's angry face and sighed, pulling her foot out of the way. 'I'm listening.'

'*And the Archbishop of Canterbury agreed to meet William and offer him the crown . . .*' Alice's sister droned on.

Alice popped the daisy chain over Dinah's

head, and giggled as it slipped over the kitten's eyes. It fell, landing on her sister's bonnet.

'Alice!' her sister snapped. 'Would you kindly pay attention to your history lesson?'

'I'm sorry, but how can one possibly pay attention to a book with no pictures?' asked Alice, looking very bored.

'My dear child,' said her sister. 'There are a great many good books in this world without pictures.'

'In this world, perhaps,' Alice murmured softly. 'But in *my* world the books would be nothing BUT pictures.'

Her sister shrugged. 'Your world!' she sniffed. 'What nonsense.'

'That's it, Dinah!' Alice whispered to the kitten. 'If I had a world of my own, *everything* would be nonsense. What it is, it wouldn't be, and what it wouldn't be, it would! You see?'

'Meow!' said Dinah, looking confused.

Alice climbed down from the tree. 'In my

2

world, you wouldn't say *meow*,' she laughed, lifting Dinah down too. 'You'd say "*Yes, Miss Alice*".'

Alice wandered away through a field of tall flowers, butterflies fluttering around her. 'In *my* world, rabbits would reside in fancy little houses. And be dressed in shoes and hats and trousers, because my world would be a wonderland . . .'

'Meow!' said Dinah. The kitten was very excited because she had just spotted a large white rabbit.

'Oh, Dinah,' Alice laughed. 'It's just a rabbit with a waistcoat.' Then her eyes opened wide in amazement. 'And a watch!'

The rabbit lifted his pocket watch and stared at it. 'Oh, my fur and whiskers!' he wailed. 'I'm late!'

Alice looked puzzled. 'Now this is curious,' she said. 'What could a rabbit possibly be late for?'

She ran after him, and Dinah followed. 'I'm late for a very important date,' the

rabbit puffed. 'No time to say hello. Goodbye! I'm late, I'm late, I'm late!'

And he ran off down the hill and into a rabbit hole in the roots of a tall tree. Alice peered into the hole.

Suddenly the floor of the hole became very steep, and Alice slipped and fell downwards.

'Goodbye, Dinah!' she called.

Chapter Two

As Alice fell, her dress ballooned out around her like a parachute, and she began to drift down the dark hole. She noticed things floating past her. There was a lamp on a table, so Alice switched it on so that she could see better. There were pictures, a mirror, a grandfather clock and a book on a table. A rocking chair floated underneath her, but as Alice sat back and relaxed the chair rocked too hard, and threw her out again.

'Goodness!' Alice gasped. 'What if I should fall right through the centre of the earth . . .' She stared at a map floating past. 'And come out the other side, where people walk upside down? Oh, but that's silly,' she went on. 'Nobody . . .'

Alice landed with a jolt, upside down. There, ahead of her, was the white rabbit, still running very quickly.

'Oh, Mr Rabbit!' she called. 'Wait! Please!'

The rabbit disappeared down the hallway, and slammed the door shut behind him. Alice rushed to open it. But she was very surprised to see another, smaller, door behind it. Behind that was an even smaller door, then another and another. Finally, Alice just managed to crawl through the smallest door into another room.

'Curiouser and curiouser,' Alice said to herself.

On the other side of the room, a curtain was flapping. Alice rushed to look. Behind the curtain was another, tiny door. Eagerly, Alice tugged at the doorknob.

The doorknob pulled a face. 'Oh!' it grumbled.

Alice was startled. 'I beg your pardon!' she gasped.

'It's quite all right,' the doorknob replied. 'But you *did* give me quite a turn!'

Alice began to explain. 'You see, I was following . . .'

'Rather good, what?' the doorknob went on. 'Doorknob. Turn. Ha, ha, ha!'

Alice waited impatiently as the doorknob chuckled at his joke.

'Well, one good turn deserves another,' the doorknob said at last. 'What can I do for you?'

'I'm looking for a white rabbit,' Alice replied. 'So if you don't mind . . .'

Alice peered through the keyhole. 'There he is!' she cried, reaching for the doorknob. 'I simply must get through!'

'Sorry, you're much too big,' the doorknob said firmly. 'Why don't you try the bottle on the table?'

'Table?' Alice repeated, glancing round.

There stood the table with a bottle on it.

The label on the bottle read *Drink Me*.

Cautiously Alice took out the cork. 'Hmm,' she muttered, 'better look first, for if one drinks too much from a bottle marked *Poison*, it's almost certain to disagree with one sooner or later.'

Alice stared hard at the bottle. At last, she took a sip.

'Tastes like cherry tart,' she said.

She didn't notice that she had started to shrink.

'Custard,' Alice went on thoughtfully.

She shrank a little more.

'Pineapple . . . roast turkey. Goodness!'

Alice was now so small that she couldn't hold the bottle.

'What did I do?' she gasped.

The doorknob was laughing. 'You almost went out like a candle!' it joked.

'But look!' Eagerly, Alice reached for the doorknob. 'I'm just the right size!'

The doorknob pulled back. 'I forgot to tell you,' it laughed, 'I'm locked!'

'Oh no!' Alice was very disappointed.

'You've got the key,' the doorknob went on.

'What key?' asked Alice.

The doorknob looked up at the glass table. 'Now don't tell me you left it up there!' it sighed.

Alice stared up at the table as a key magically appeared. She tried to climb up the table leg, but slid back down again. 'Whatever will I do?'

'Try the box,' remarked the doorknob.

At that very moment a box appeared at Alice's feet. She reached in and pulled out a biscuit.

'*Eat me*,' Alice read. 'All right. But goodness knows what this will do!'

Alice sat on the floor and began nibbling at the biscuit. Straight away she started to grow. And grow. She grew so big that her head thudded against the ceiling.

'A little of that went a long way!' the doorknob laughed.

9

'Well, I don't think it's so funny,' said Alice miserably, and she began to cry.

'Come now,' the doorknob said. 'Crying won't help.'

'I know,' Alice gulped. 'But I just can't seem to stop . . .'

'This won't do at all,' the doorknob spluttered as Alice's tears began to fill the little room.

Alice saw the bottle bobbing about on the sea of tears. She grabbed it and drank, shrinking as quickly as she had grown. She became so tiny that she fell inside the bottle.

'Oh dear!' Alice groaned. 'I do wish I hadn't cried so much.'

The bottle bobbed towards the door. It floated through the keyhole, into darkness.

Peering through the bottle, Alice saw a very strange sight. A large dodo was sailing across the water on top of a toucan, and an eagle was pushing them along like a sail.

'Ahoy!' called the dodo. 'Land ho!'

'Oh, Mr Dodo!' Alice shouted. 'Please help me!'

As she spoke, she leaned out too far. The bottle tipped up, and filled with water.

Meanwhile, the birds had reached land, and the toucan and the eagle began to run a very strange race around the dodo, which was perched on a rock. There was no beginning and no end to the race, no winners and no losers.

Alice struggled to get out of the bottle. At last, soaking wet all over, she was cast up on the beach.

'You'll never get dry that way,' the dodo called. 'You have to run with the others.'

Just as Alice was being pushed round and round the rock by the birds, she saw him.

'The White Rabbit!' she gasped.

Chapter Three

The White Rabbit was swirling around on the waves in an umbrella filled with water.

'Oh, Mr Rabbit!' Alice yelled.

'Oh, my goodness,' the rabbit muttered, as the umbrella whirled up on to the beach. 'I'm late, I'm late.' He jumped out of the umbrella, and ran towards a clump of trees. Alice followed. As she searched for him among the trees, she didn't notice two plump, round boys dancing behind her, trying to attract her attention. They looked exactly the same, with the same caps and blue bow ties.

'I wonder . . .' Alice murmured, crawling inside a hollow log.

The two boys danced along the log, and hopped off the other end. When Alice climbed out, she jumped backwards, and stared at the two boys. 'Oh, what peculiar little figures!'

One of the boys had *Tweedledee* embroidered on his collar and the other had *Tweedledum*. Alice poked Tweedledee in the stomach and he let out a *beep*.

'If you think we're waxworks, you ought to pay, you know,' he said.

'Contrariwise, if you think we're alive,' said Tweedledum, 'you ought to speak to us.'

'Well,' Alice laughed, turning away, 'it's been nice meeting you.'

Immediately the twins rushed round to block Alice's path.

'You're beginning backwards,' Tweedledee said.

'The first thing in a visit is to say how do you do!' Tweedledum reminded her.

'That's manners!' they said together, looking sternly at Alice.

'Well, my name is Alice, and I'm following a white rabbit,' explained Alice. 'So . . .'

And she tried to walk away, but the twins headed her off again.

'Oh, you can't go yet,' Tweedledum said firmly.

'No, the visit has just started,' Tweedledee agreed.

'That's very kind of you,' Alice replied politely. 'But I must be going, because I'm following a white rabbit.'

'Why?' the twins asked together.

'Well – er –' Alice stammered. 'I'm curious to know where he's going.'

'Oh, she's curious!' Tweedledum repeated.

The twins tutted sadly, and shook their heads.

'The oysters were curious, too,' Tweedledee whispered.

'Poor things!' the twins sighed together.

'Why, what happened to the oysters?' Alice wanted to know.

'Oh, you wouldn't be interested,' said Tweedledee airily.

'But I am!' Alice replied.

14

The twins immediately grabbed Alice, and sat her down on the log.

'*The Walrus and the Carpenter*,' Tweedledee announced.

'Or, *The Story of the Curious Oysters*,' added Tweedledum.

The twins began to tell Alice a very long poem about the Walrus and his friend, the Carpenter, who were walking on the beach. There they found an oyster bed, and they charmed all the little oysters out of their shells. The curious oysters followed them, and ended up becoming the Walrus and the Carpenter's dinner.

'That was a very sad story,' Alice sighed. 'Well, it's been a very nice visit . . .' She got up but the twins pushed her down again.

'Another recitation, entitled *Father William*,' Tweedledee announced. '*You are old, Father William, the young man said* . . .'

The twins began to dance around the trees, and this time Alice managed to slip away without being seen.

Chapter Four

Soon Alice came to a very neat little house with pink shutters at the windows.

'Now I wonder who lives here?' Alice said to herself.

'Mary Ann!' shouted a voice inside the house. 'Drat that girl! Where could she have put them?'

The shutters flew open and the White Rabbit's head popped out. 'Mary Ann!'

'The rabbit!' Alice said with delight, pushing open the gate.

'I'm awfully late,' the rabbit groaned, closing the shutters. Suddenly the door burst open, and the rabbit dashed out.

'Why, Mary Ann!' the rabbit said crossly, peering at her closely in a very short-sighted way. 'What are you doing out here?'

Alice looked puzzled. 'Mary Ann?' she repeated.

'Don't just do something,' the rabbit ordered her, bouncing around impatiently. 'Stand there! No, no, get my gloves!' He ushered Alice into the house. 'At once! Do you hear?'

'Goodness!' Alice remarked, as she walked upstairs. 'I suppose I'll be taking orders from Dinah next.'

Alice crossed the room, and looked at the dressing table. 'Hmm, now let me see,' she murmured, opening the drawers. 'If I were a rabbit, where would I keep my gloves?'

She lifted the lid off a biscuit jar, and peeped in. The jar was filled with biscuits, and the top one read *Eat Me*.

'Thank you,' Alice said politely. 'I don't mind if I do.'

Humming, she ate the biscuit and then walked over to a large trunk. But as she looked inside for the gloves, she began to grow.

'Oh, no, not again!' Alice wailed, as her head hit the roof with a thump.

Outside the rabbit was getting very cross. He raced inside, and up the stairs. As he opened the door, a giant foot came out and pushed him downstairs.

'H – E – L – P!' the rabbit yelped.

Alice's foot came after him. It pushed the rabbit out of the front door, and into the greenhouse which stood in the garden.

Poor Alice was now so big that her arms and legs stuck out of all the windows.

'Help!' squeaked the rabbit, climbing out of his broken greenhouse. 'Monster! In my house, Dodo!'

'Dodo?' Alice repeated.

The dodo and the rabbit were hurrying towards the house.

'Oh, my poor little house,' wailed the rabbit.

'Steady, old chap,' the dodo boomed.

18

'Can't be as bad as all that, you know.'

The rabbit pointed at Alice. 'There it is!' he cried.

'By Jove!' the dodo exclaimed, looking quite startled.

'Do something!' the rabbit shouted, and pushed his friend through the gate.

The dodo walked up to Alice's foot, and examined it. 'I have a very simple solution,' he announced.

Alice peered out of one of the upstairs windows. 'Thank goodness,' she sighed.

'Simply pull it out of the chimney,' the dodo went on.

'Go on!' the rabbit cried eagerly. 'Pull it out!'

The dodo shrugged. 'Who, me?' he replied. 'Don't be ridiculous! What we need is . . .'

At that moment a lizard came along. He was carrying a broom and a ladder.

'A lizard with a ladder!' the dodo finished off.

19

'Oh, Bill!' the rabbit called. 'We need a lazard with a lizard – uh, can you help us?'

'At your service, guv'nor,' the lizard replied cheerfully.

The dodo began pushing Bill up the ladder. 'You just pop down the chimney, and send that monster out of there.'

'Right-oh, guv'nor,' Bill agreed. But when he peered in through the window and saw Alice's huge eyes staring back at him, he let out a shriek.

'Monster! Wow!'

Bill turned and fled. But the dodo and the rabbit ran after him, and pulled him back.

'Steady now,' the dodo boomed. 'Bill, lad, you're passing up a golden opportunity.'

'I am?' Bill repeated.

'You can be famous!' the dodo declared, carrying Bill up the ladder. He began to push the lizard down the chimney. 'In you go now. Simply tie your tail round the monster's neck, and drag it out.'

Inside the room, Alice could see soot falling down the chimney into the fireplace. The soot was tickling her nose.

'Ah – ah – ah – AH – CHOO!'

Alice sneezed loudly. Bill the lizard shot back up the chimney like a ball from a cannon, and flew high up into the sky.

'Well, there goes Bill!' remarked the dodo, taking out his pipe.

Alice glanced out of the window. 'Poor Bill,' she sighed.

The dodo had another bright idea. 'We'll smoke the blighter out,' he sang.

He hurried into the house, and began carrying out clocks and cupboards and other bits of furniture to make a bonfire.

'Oh, me, oh, my,' the rabbit sobbed. 'My poor house and furniture.'

As Alice watched anxiously from the windows, the dodo lit the bonfire. Smoke began to curl upwards.

'Oh dear,' Alice murmured. 'This is serious.' She thought for a minute. 'Perhaps

21

if I ate something, it would make me grow smaller . . .'

Alice reached into the garden to take a carrot from the vegetable patch. The rabbit rushed over to stop her, but Alice picked him up along with the carrot.

'I'm sorry,' she told the frightened rabbit, 'but I must eat something.'

'Not me!' shrieked the rabbit, getting the wrong idea. 'You – you barbarian!'

Alice began to shrink. She dropped the rabbit and he dashed out of the room.

Outside the dodo was still blowing on the fire to get it started. The rabbit glanced at his watch.

'Oh no, must go!' The rabbit shook hands with the dodo, and ran off. Meanwhile, Alice had come downstairs, and slipped outside under the front door.

'Wait!' she called. 'Mr Rabbit!'

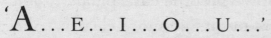

Chapter Five

'A . . . E . . . I . . . O . . . U . . .'

Alice could hear someone talking. She stopped and peeped out from behind some leaves.

'A . . . E . . . I . . . O . . . U . . .'

A large blue caterpillar was sitting on a mushroom. He was smoking a pipe, and blowing smoke shapes into the air.

'O . . . U . . . E . . . I . . . O . . .' he chanted lazily.

Feeling curious, Alice climbed up on to a smaller mushroom to get a better look.

'Whooo . . . are . . . yooou?' the caterpillar asked slowly, blowing smoke rings with each word.

'Why,' Alice said sadly, 'I hardly know,

sir. I've changed so many times since this morning, you see.'

'I do *not* see,' the caterpillar replied. 'Explain yourself.'

'I'm afraid I can't explain myself,' Alice went on, 'because I'm not myself, you know.'

'I do *not* know,' said the caterpillar.

'Well, I can't put it any more clearly,' Alice sighed, 'for it isn't clear to me.'

The caterpillar blew a U-shaped smoke ring. 'You? Who are *you*?'

'Don't you think you ought to tell me who you are first?' asked Alice, dodging the smoke.

'Why?' the caterpillar wanted to know.

Gloomily Alice sat down on the mushroom. 'Oh dear,' she sighed, 'everything is so confusing.'

The caterpillar blew out another smoke ring. 'Whooo . . . are . . . yooou?'

As the smoke swirled around her head, Alice began to cough and sneeze. Very annoyed, she turned and walked off.

'You there, girl, wait!' the caterpillar called after her.

Alice peered out from behind a blade of grass.

'Come back,' ordered the caterpillar. 'I have something important to say.'

She looked up at the caterpillar. 'Well?'

The caterpillar lay on his back, blowing smoke rings. 'Keep your temper,' he said smugly.

'Is that all?' Alice snapped.

'What is your problem?' asked the caterpillar.

'Well,' Alice said, 'I should like to be a little larger, sir. Three inches is such a wretched height.'

The caterpillar jumped up angrily. 'I am exactly three inches high,' he snorted furiously. 'And it is a very good height indeed.' He then puffed on his pipe so fiercely that he turned purple and disappeared in clouds of smoke. All that was left on the mushroom was his pipe.

'By the way, I have a few more helpful hints . . .' came the caterpillar's voice from above. Alice looked up. A blue butterfly was fluttering overhead.

'One side will make you grow taller,' the butterfly said, flying higher. 'And the other side will make you grow shorter.'

'THE OTHER SIDE OF WHAT?' shouted Alice.

The butterfly swooped back towards her. 'The mushroom, of course,' and it flew away.

'Hmm,' Alice said thoughtfully. She broke a piece from each side of the mushroom and she took a bite from one of the pieces. 'I'm tired of being only three inches high.'

Suddenly Alice shot up higher and higher. She grew so fast, that in only a few seconds her head was up by the top of the trees. On the way up she dislodged a bird's nest, which sat on her head like a hat.

'Help!' The mother bird flew out of the nest, looking terrified. 'A serpent! Help!'

'But I'm not a serpent!' Alice cried.

'I'm late for a very important date!' the White Rabbit puffed.

'Oh, you can't go yet,' Tweedledum said firmly.

'But of course we can talk, my dear!'

'Whooo...are...you?' the caterpillar asked slowly.

'I'm just a little girl!' pleaded Alice.

'Most everyone's mad here,' the Cheshire Cat grinned.

'Oh no, my watch!' wailed the White Rabbit.

The Queen readied herself to swing her flamingo,
while Alice tried to control hers.

'OFF WITH HER HEAD!' yelled the Queen.

Wonderland had all been a dream . . .

'Indeed!' the bird said, still looking suspicious. 'Then, just what are you?'

'I'm just a little girl,' explained Alice.

'Little!' the bird repeated scornfully. She perched on Alice's nose. 'And I suppose you don't eat eggs either?'

'Yes,' Alice admitted. 'I do.'

'I knew it!' the bird shrieked. 'Serpent!'

Alice ducked as the bird flew round her head. 'Oh, for goodness sake!' she said. She took a bite from the other piece of mushroom.

Straightaway Alice started to shrink. The nest fell off her head and landed on a branch as she got smaller and smaller. Soon she was tiny again.

Alice sighed. 'I wonder if I'll ever get the knack of it.'

This time she licked the piece of mushroom instead of biting it. She grew up a little way, and stopped.

'There!' Alice looked pleased with herself. 'That's much better. I'd better save these.'

She put the pieces of mushroom in her pocket, and set off again. At the crossroads stood a tall tree covered in signs. Alice stopped to read them. 'I wonder which way I ought to go?' she said.

'*'Twas brillig and the slithy toves did gyre and gimbel in the wabe . . .*'

Someone was singing a nonsense song. Alice looked round. Suddenly the forest seemed full of strange lights which shone and flickered.

'Lose something?' purred the voice.

Frightened, Alice jumped back and looked up into the tree. All she could see were two rows of shining white teeth.

'Oh!' she gasped, as two eyes and a mouth appeared. Then, slowly, a pink and purple striped body came into view.

'Why!' Alice exclaimed. 'You're a cat!'

'A Cheshire Cat!' he purred, and began to disappear again.

'Oh, don't go, please!' Alice cried. 'I just wanted to ask you which way I should go.'

'Well, that depends on where you want to get to,' the cat replied.

'It really doesn't matter,' Alice began.

'Then it really doesn't matter which way you go,' retorted the cat, and he jumped off the branch, disappearing into thin air. The next moment, paw prints began to appear on the ground, walking around Alice.

'If you'd really like to know,' the cat went on, jumping into the tree again, 'he went *that* way.'

Puzzled, Alice looked round. 'Who did?' she asked.

'The White Rabbit,' purred the cat.

Alice's face lit up. 'He did?'

'He did what?' asked the cat.

Alice pointed. 'Went that way.'

'Who did?'

Alice was getting annoyed. 'The White Rabbit!'

The Cheshire Cat was standing on his head. 'If I were looking for a white rabbit,' he purred, 'I'd ask the Mad Hatter.'

Alice looked nervous. 'The *Mad* Hatter?'

'Or there's the March Hare.' The Cheshire Cat pointed out the way. 'In that direction.'

'Oh, thank you,' Alice smiled. 'I think I shall visit him.'

'Of course, he's mad too,' the cat remarked.

'But I don't want to go amongst mad people!' Alice said anxiously.

The Cheshire Cat smiled widely. 'Oh, you can't help that,' he chuckled. 'Most everyone's mad here.' His body began to fade, leaving nothing behind but his stripes. 'You may have noticed that I'm not all there myself!'

Chapter Six

'*A very merry unbirthday to us, to us!*'

Alice could hear loud singing as she walked towards the March Hare's house. A very strange tea party was taking place under the trees. There was a long table set with food and lots of teapots which were blowing out clouds of steam.

Alice watched in amazement as the Mad Hatter pulled a dormouse from one of the teapots. Then she clapped her hands as the song finished.

The Mad Hatter and the March Hare stared at Alice. Then they jumped up and scurried along the table towards her shouting, 'No room! No room!'

'But I thought there was plenty of room,'

Alice said firmly, sitting down in an empty chair.

'Oh, but it's very rude to sit down without being invited,' the March Hare scolded.

'It's very rude indeed,' the Mad Hatter agreed.

The dormouse lifted the lid of the teapot. 'Very, very rude indeed!' he muttered before sinking back down to sleep.

'Oh, I'm very sorry,' Alice said. 'But I did enjoy your singing.'

'You enjoyed our singing?' the March Hare broke in.

'Oh, what a delightful child,' the Mad Hatter beamed. 'You must have a cup of tea.'

'That would be very nice.' Alice sat down. 'I'm sorry I interrupted your birthday party.'

'My dear child,' laughed the March Hare, 'this is *not* a birthday party.'

'This is an *unbirthday* party,' the Mad Hatter giggled.

Alice looked puzzled. 'I don't quite understand,' she said.

The March Hare began to play a tune on the teapots, and the Mad Hatter stood up, one foot on the table.

'Now,' he announced, 'statistics prove that you've one birthday every year. But there are three hundred and sixty-four *unbirthdays*!'

Excited, Alice jumped up from her chair. 'Why, then today is my unbirthday, too!' The March Hare and the Mad Hatter began to dance around Alice singing '*A very merry unbirthday to you!*'

'Oh, that was lovely!' she laughed.

The Mad Hatter seated himself at the table again. 'You were saying that you were seeking information of some kind?' He dunked his saucer in a cup of tea, and chewed on it.

'Well,' Alice began, 'it all started when I was sitting on the river bank with Dinah . . .'

The March Hare interrupted her. 'I have an excellent idea,' he announced. 'Let's

change the subject. How about a nice cup of tea?'

Alice was annoyed. 'Well, I'm sorry,' she said crossly, 'but I just haven't the time.'

'No time, no time, no time!' called a voice Alice knew.

It was the White Rabbit. He waved at them as he hurried past.

'I'm late, I'm late,' he muttered, pulling out his watch.

The Mad Hatter grabbed the watch and shook it.

'Well, no wonder you're late,' he said scornfully. 'This clock is exactly two days slow.'

'Two days slow?' the White Rabbit gasped.

The Mad Hatter dipped the watch into the teapot, opened it, poured salt inside and flicked out all the cogs and wheels with a fork. Then he spread butter on the watch with a knife.

'Oh, no, no!' wailed the White Rabbit.

The Mad Hatter poured tea on to the watch, added some sugar and spread it with jam. 'That should do it!' he announced.

The watch exploded.

'Oh dear!' the White Rabbit groaned, as the Mad Hatter passed him the broken watch. Then he and the March Hare picked the rabbit up and heaved him over the wall.

'Of all the silly nonsense!' Alice said, disgusted. 'That is the stupidest tea party I've ever been to in my whole life.' She set off through the woods again. 'I'm going home. Straight home!'

Chapter Seven

Alice marched back the way she had come.

'That rabbit!' she said to herself. 'Who cares where he's going, anyway?'

She stopped as she saw a sign in front of her which read *Tulgey Wood*.

'Curious,' said Alice. 'I don't remember *this*. Now let me see . . .'

A strange-looking bird, shaped like a pair of glasses, hopped on to the sign, then on to Alice's nose. A bird shaped like a mirror joined them. Alice looked at herself in the mirror bird, and saw the glasses bird on her nose. Quickly she put the mirror bird down.

'No more nonsense!' she said firmly.

The eyes of both birds followed Alice as she went on her way.

'Goodness!' she said. 'When I get home, I shall write a book about this place!' She looked around, worried. 'If I – if I ever *do* get home . . .'

Suddenly little furry creatures were springing up around her feet. They scuttled into an arrow-shape, which pointed to a path.

'Oh, thank goodness!' Alice exclaimed. 'If I hurry, perhaps I might even be home in time for tea.' But ahead of Alice, a dog, shaped like a broom, was busy brushing the path away. Alice watched in horror as the dog brushed and brushed, until only the tiny bit of path she was standing on was left. Feeling very sad and lost, she sat down on a rock and began to cry.

A lazy voice purred from a nearby tree.

Alice looked up. 'Oh, Cheshire Cat, it's you!' she gulped. 'I want to go home, but I can't find my way.'

'Naturally,' the Cheshire Cat agreed. 'That's because you *have* no way. All ways here, you see, are the Queen's ways.'

'But I've never met any queen,' said Alice.

'You haven't?' The Cheshire Cat looked very surprised. 'Oh, but you must. She'll be mad about you!' And he laughed.

'How can I find her?' Alice asked eagerly.

'Well,' the cat purred, 'some go this way, some go that way. But as for me myself, I prefer the short cut . . .'

The Cheshire Cat pulled a lever, and a door swung open in the trunk of the tree.

Chapter Eight

Alice peered through the opening. A path lay ahead of her, and she skipped down it, wondering where it would lead her. Suddenly a drop of red paint came flying over the hedge, and splashed at her feet.

Alice could hear singing. *'We're painting the roses red, we're painting the roses red!'*

She ran over to the hedge, and saw three playing cards dancing around a rosebush. One was a Three, one a Two and one an Ace. They were painting the white roses red. When they'd finished, they started on the next bush.

'Oh, pardon me,' called Alice, looking very puzzled. 'But, Mr Three, *why* must you paint them red?'

The cards looked very worried.

'Well, the fact is, miss,' said the Three, slapping on more red paint, 'we planted white roses by mistake, and the Queen, she likes them red. If she saw white instead . . .'

'She'd raise a fuss,' chimed in the Ace.

'And each of us –' muttered the Two.

'Would quickly lose his head!' finished the Three.

'Goodness!' Alice said, very shocked. 'Then let me help you.' She picked up a paintbrush, and joined in the song.

Suddenly, there was a loud fanfare of trumpets.

'The Queen!' yelled the three cards. They dropped their buckets of paint, and threw themselves down on the ground. Alice thought she'd better do the same.

A grand procession of cards was marching its way towards them.

'Cards – HALT!' shouted the commander.

Then, to Alice's surprise, the White Rabbit bustled forwards, blowing a horn. 'Her

Imperial Highness,' the rabbit panted. 'Her Grace, Her Royal Majesty, the Queen of Hearts!'

The Queen of Hearts was big and round, with a very bad-tempered face. But at the moment she was smiling sweetly and nodding at her subjects.

'Hurray!' called the cards loudly.

A very small King of Hearts appeared from behind the Queen's skirts, and tapped the rabbit on the shoulder.

'And the King,' mumbled the rabbit.

The King bowed, but this time only one person cheered. Meanwhile, the Queen began to walk past her card soldiers. She touched one of the painted roses and a look of fury crossed her face.

'Who's been painting my roses red?' she roared. She ripped the rosebush up by its roots, and shook it. 'WHO'S BEEN PAINTING MY ROSES RED?' She stared down accusingly at the three cards next to Alice. 'Off with their heads!'

The crowd cheered. Alice watched in dismay as the three cards were carried away by some of the soldiers.

'Oh, please,' Alice whispered, looking up at her. 'They were only trying to –'

The Queen pointed at Alice. 'And who is *this*?' she asked.

The King looked Alice over. 'Well,' he began, 'now let me see, my dear. It certainly isn't a Heart.'

The Queen bent closer to Alice. 'Why, it's a little girl,' she said sweetly. 'Now, where do you come from, and where are you going?'

'Well,' Alice explained, 'I'm trying to find my way home.'

'Your way!' the Queen bellowed angrily. 'All ways here are MY ways!'

'Yes, Your Majesty,' Alice agreed quickly, 'but I was only going to ask –'

'I'll ask the questions,' the Queen growled. 'Do you play croquet?'

'Why, yes, Your Majesty,' said Alice.

'Then let the game begin!' shouted the Queen.

The rabbit blew his trumpet again. Cards began sailing through the air and landing on the lawn to form hoops. The rabbit rushed over, carrying a bag of pink flamingo croquet clubs, and the Queen chose one. Then a hedgehog, curled into a tight ball, was placed at her feet.

Alice tried to choose a flamingo for herself, but they flapped and squawked loudly.

'SILENCE!' roared the Queen. She swung her flamingo at the hedgehog, but missed. Quickly the King rushed over, and gave the hedgehog a poke to send him on his way.

The hedgehog rolled off down the lawn. The cards jumped in front of him, making sure he rolled through the hoops. The crowd cheered loudly, and the Queen looked smug.

But the last card didn't get into place quickly enough. He stumbled and fell, and everyone looked horrified.

'Off with his head!' shouted the Queen. 'Next!' And she bowed to Alice.

Feeling rather nervous, Alice tried to hit her hedgehog with the flamingo. But the flamingo kept trying to fly away. At last, she got the bird in place, and managed to roll her hedgehog along the lawn.

The Queen looked worried. But the cards moved their feet and flattened themselves down and jumped out of the way, so that Alice didn't score any points. The Queen grinned widely, but Alice was disgusted.

As the Queen walked off to take her next shot, Alice heard the sound of humming. There, sitting on the bustle of the Queen's dress, was the Cheshire Cat.

'I say, how are you getting on?' he purred.

'Not at all!' Alice snapped.

The cat smiled and disappeared, appearing again on the Queen's shoulder.

'Who *are* you talking to?' the Queen asked Alice.

'A cat, Your Majesty.' Alice pointed at

the Queen's shoulder, but the cat had disappeared. Now it appeared again under her left arm.

'What cat?' the Queen demanded.

'There!' Alice pointed, but the cat was behind the Queen, on her bustle again.

'I warn you, child,' the Queen snarled, 'if I lose my temper, you lose your head! Understand?'

'You know, we could make her really angry,' the Cheshire Cat remarked to Alice. 'Shall we try?'

'Oh, no!' Alice begged.

The Queen was holding her flamingo, ready to take her next shot. The Cheshire Cat grabbed the flamingo, and hooked its beak under the Queen's dress.

'No!' Alice cried.

The Queen swung the flamingo, and flung herself up into the air and across the grass. She landed in a tangled heap. Horrified, Alice clapped her hand over her mouth.

'Oh, my fur and whiskers!' moaned the White Rabbit.

'Oh dear!' groaned the King.

The Queen picked herself up, her face red with rage. 'Someone's head will roll for this!' she bellowed. She pointed at Alice. 'YOURS!'

'Oh, but –' the King interrupted her nervously, 'couldn't she have a trial first?'

The Queen patted him on the head. 'Very well, then,' she agreed. 'Let the trial begin!'

Chapter Nine

Alice stood in the prisoner's dock in the courtroom. The Queen of Hearts sat on the judge's bench, and all the card soldiers were lined up around the room.

'Your Majesty,' the White Rabbit announced, 'members of the jury, loyal subjects –' The King tapped him on the shoulder. 'And the King. The prisoner at the bar is charged with enticing Her Majesty the Queen of Hearts into a game of croquet, and teasing, tormenting and otherwise annoying our beloved and –'

'Never mind all that!' the Queen burst out furiously. 'Get to the part where I lose my temper!'

'Thereby causing the Queen to lose her

temper!' the White Rabbit finished quickly.

The Queen looked pleased. 'Now,' she smiled sweetly at Alice. 'Are you ready for your sentence?'

'Oh, but there must be a verdict first!' Alice protested.

'Sentence first!' The Queen banged her fist on the bench. 'Verdict afterwards! Off with her –'

'But consider, my dear,' the King broke in. 'We've called no witnesses. Couldn't we hear maybe one or two?'

'Oh, very well,' the Queen muttered. 'But get on with it!'

'First witness,' cried the King. 'The March Hare.'

Two cards brought the March Hare to the witness box. He was holding a cup and saucer.

'And what do you know about this unfortunate affair?' the King asked him.

'Nothing,' replied the March Hare.

'Nothing whatever?' the Queen repeated.

'That's very important. Jury, write that down! Next witness!'

'The Dormouse,' called the White Rabbit.

Two cards carried a teapot into the courtroom. The Queen removed the lid, and peered in.

'What have you to say about this?' she asked the dormouse.

'Twinkle, twinkle, little bat,' said the dormouse drowsily, and dropped back into the teapot.

'That's the most important piece of evidence we've heard yet,' the Queen announced.

The Mad Hatter jumped up on top of the witness box.

'Off with your hat!' roared the Queen.

The Mad Hatter removed his top hat, revealing a teapot and a cup and saucer balanced on his head.

'And where were you when this horrible crime was committed?' asked the King.

'I was at home, drinking tea,' the Mad

Hatter explained. 'You know, it's my unbirthday.'

The King turned to the Queen. 'Why, my dear,' he said, 'today is *your* unbirthday, too!'

Straightaway, the Mad Hatter and March Hare unrolled a tablecloth, producing teapots, cups and saucers and a cake.

'*A very merry unbirthday to you!*' they sang.

The Queen blew out the candles, and the cake exploded. When the smoke cleared, there was a large hatbox. Eagerly the Queen tore it open, revealing a golden crown. Beaming, she placed it on her head.

'Oh, Your Majesty!' Alice gasped, as she saw the Cheshire Cat begin to appear on top of the crown. 'Look, there he is now!'

'Where?' the Queen asked. 'Who?'

'The Cheshire Cat!' cried Alice.

The lid shot off the teapot.

'Cat!' squeaked the dormouse in terror. He scrambled out of the teapot, and ran off.

'Help!' shouted the Mad Hatter. 'Stop him!'

The dormouse climbed up a tapestry hanging on the wall. The Mad Hatter and the March Hare followed him, knocking the Queen from her bench.

'Somebody's head will roll for this!' the Queen shouted furiously, glaring at Alice.

Suddenly Alice remembered what she had in her pocket. Quickly Alice popped both pieces of mushroom in her mouth. Immediately she began to grow.

'Off with her –' the Queen began again, but then she looked scared as Alice shot right up, and bumped her head against the courtroom roof.

'Oh, pooh!' Alice retorted. 'I'm not afraid of you!' She reached down and grabbed a handful of the card soldiers. 'Why, you're nothing but a pack of cards!'

Chapter Ten

'All persons more than a mile high must leave the court immediately!' called the King in a trembling voice.

'I am not a mile high,' Alice snapped, 'and I'm not leaving!'

The Queen laughed nervously as Alice stooped over them, and tried to hide herself behind the King.

'And as for you,' Alice went on, 'you're not a Queen. You're just a fat, pompous, bad-tempered –'

Alice was shrinking again, but she was so busy scolding the Queen that she didn't realize.

'– old tyrant!' Alice finished.

The Queen looked pleased, as Alice glanced

down at herself in horror. She was tiny.

'What were you saying, my dear?' she asked smoothly.

'Well,' said the Cheshire Cat, leaning down from his perch on the Queen's crown, 'she simply said that you're a fat, pompous, bad-tempered, old tyrant!'

And he faded away, laughing.

'OFF WITH HER HEAD!' shouted the Queen.

The card soldiers tried to trap Alice, but she ran as fast as she could, out of the palace and into the garden maze. The cards, the King, the Queen and the White Rabbit followed her.

The maze twisted and turned in all directions. Suddenly the card soldiers caught up with Alice. They lifted her up and threw her into the air.

Suddenly, magically, Alice was back on the beach, and the race without end was still taking place. This time the King, the Queen and the card army were taking part, too.

'Here we go again,' they sang. 'No one ever loses, and no one can ever win!'

Alice ran off along the beach. Behind her she could hear the Queen yelling, 'Off with her head!'

Suddenly the beach changed into a long table. Alice ran along it, hopping over the teapots. The Mad Hatter and the March Hare popped up and grabbed her.

'You must join us in a cup of tea!' The March Hare and the Mad Hatter pulled Alice up on to the handle of a large teaspoon, which rested against a giant cup. The spoon tipped, and all three of them fell into the tea.

Alice began to swim. She came up to the surface, and there was the Queen being pushed across the water by the toucan and the eagle. 'Off with her head!' the Queen shouted.

A mushroom floated past, and on it sat the caterpillar, smoking his pipe. Panting, Alice swam over and held on to the edge of the mushroom. 'Mr Caterpillar,' she cried, 'what shall I do?'

The caterpillar blew out smoke. 'Who are *you*?'

Alice disappeared in a cloud of smoke. The smoke turned into a tunnel, and Alice was running down it as fast as she could. The Queen and the card soldiers were chasing after her.

'Don't let her get away!' roared the Queen. 'Off with her head!'

A door was floating around ahead of Alice. She tried desperately to grab the doorknob, but it kept drifting out of reach. At last she caught it.

'Ouch!' said the doorknob. 'Still locked, you know!'

'I simply must get out!' Alice gasped, tugging at the knob.

The doorknob laughed. 'But you *are* outside!'

Alice stared through the keyhole. She
could see herself leaning against a tree, fast
asleep. Dinah lay in her lap.

'Don't let her get away!' the Queen
shouted.

'Alice, wake up!' called Alice. 'Please wake
up!'

The King, the Queen, the card soldiers,
the Mad Hatter, the March Hare and
everyone else began to spin round in a haze
of bright colours.

'Alice! Will you kindly pay attention
and recite your lesson!'

'Huh?' Alice woke up. 'Oh!' she gasped.
Wonderland had all been a dream . . .

'Well, come along,' sighed her sister.
'It's time for tea.'

And, yawning, Alice picked up her kitten,
and followed her sister home.

Disney

More of Disney's classic stories to collect.

Magical books to read forever.

Available to buy through your local bookshop.